THIS BOOK BELONGS TO

MAijA

THE PRINCESS AND THE PEA

Written by Helen Anderton

Illustrated by Stuart Lynch

make
believe
ideas

Reading together

This book is designed to be fun for children who are gaining confidence in their reading. They will enjoy and benefit from some time discussing the story with an adult. Here are some ways you can help your child take those first steps in reading:

* Encourage your child to look at the pictures and talk about what is happening in the story.

* Help your child to find familiar words and sound out the letters in harder words.

* Ask your child to read and repeat each short sentence.

Look at rhymes

Many of the sentences in this book are simple rhymes. Encourage your child to recognize rhyming words. Try asking the following questions:

* What does this word say?

* Can you find a word that rhymes with it?

* Look at the ending of two words that rhyme. Are they spelled the same? For example, "life" and "wife," and "pea" and "me."

Reading activities

The **What happens next?** activity encourages your child to retell the story and point to the mixed-up pictures in the right order.

The **Rhyming words** activity takes six words from the story and asks your child to read and find other words that rhyme with them.

The **Key words** pages provide practice with common words used in the context of the book. Read the sentences with your child and encourage him or her to make up more sentences using the key words listed around the border.

A **Picture dictionary** page asks children to focus closely on nine words from the story. Encourage your child to look carefully at each word, cover it with his or her hand, write it on a separate piece of paper, and finally, check it!

Do not complete all the activities at once – doing one each time you read will ensure that your child continues to enjoy the story and the time you are spending together. Have fun!

To live a very happy life,
Prince Lee must find a royal wife.
But his mom, the queen, is tough –
no girl she meets is good enough!

Each day, the queen goes out to see
    if she can find a match for Lee.
A girl must pass one hundred tests
    to prove that she's a true princess.

"This girl has chewed her fingernails.
    This one doesn't sing – she WAILS!
This girl hasn't brushed her teeth.
    Goodness me! What smelly feet!"

"We need a princess," says the queen,
  "who's pretty, fragile, sweet, and CLEAN!"
The prince says, "Yes, Mom, I agree,
  these girls aren't good enough for me!"

That night, the pair get quite a shock
when from the door, they hear a KNOCK!
They peep out through the windowpane
and see a princess in the rain.

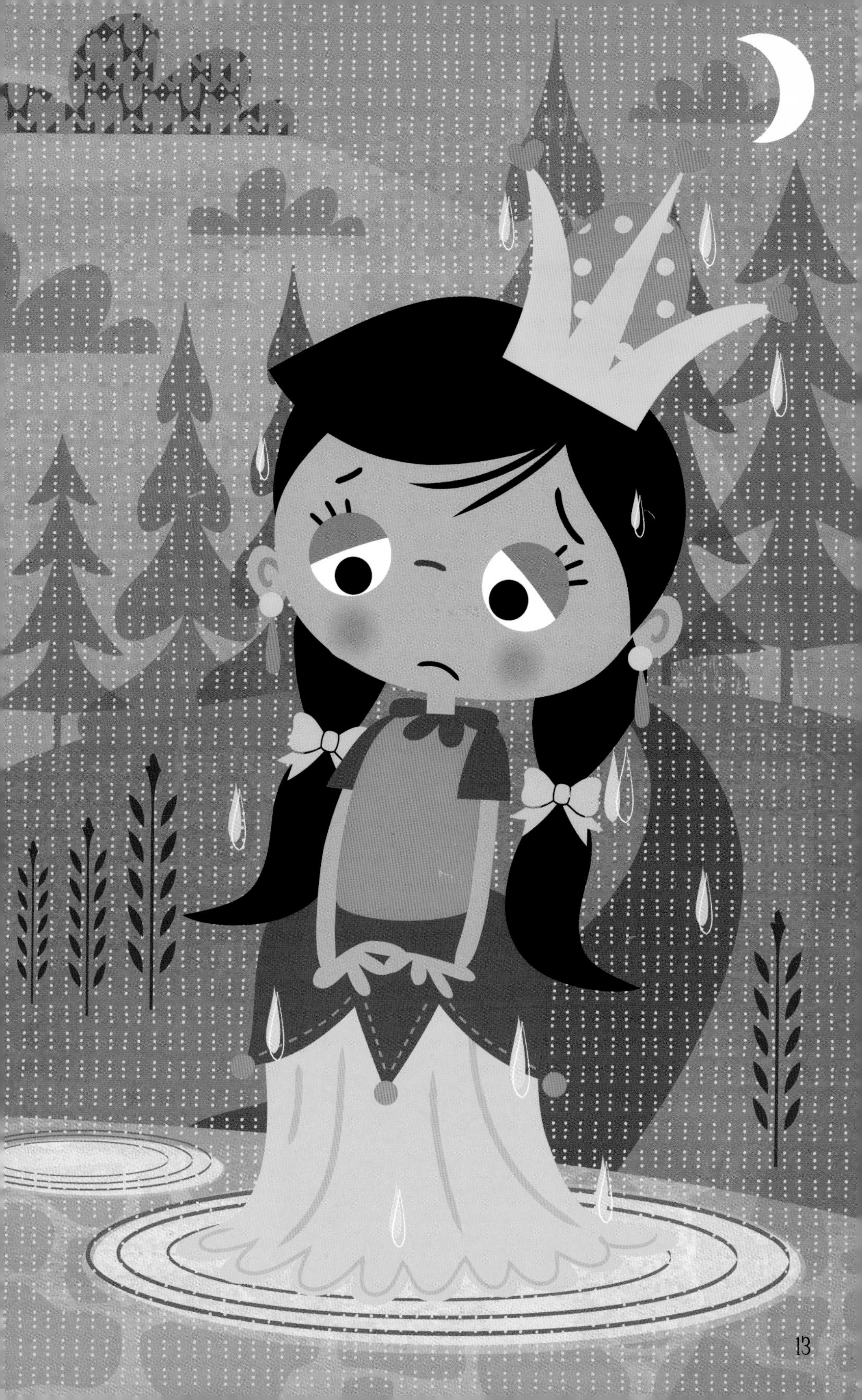

"She looks well-groomed, so let her in!"
shouts Prince Lee with an eager grin.
The girl says, "Hi, I'm Princess Dee.
Would you spare a bed for me?"

The prince says, "She's the best we've seen."
   The queen says, "All right – she looks clean!
Let's put her through a few quick tests
   to prove that she's a true princess!"

All dried out, the
girl looks great:

she has good manners;
she sits up straight;

each song she sings
is such a treat –

she even has
nice-smelling feet!

Prince Lee declares, "Dee is the one!"
      "One last test, though!" says his mom.
"Eighty soft layers make the bed
      upon which Dee will rest her head."

"Then underneath all of that fluff,
      we'll put a pea that's strong enough
to bruise a princess who is true
      and good enough to marry you!"

With fingers crossed, Lee says good-night
and tucks Dee into bed so tight.
He thinks, "That girl is just the best –
I hope she is a true princess!"

The next day, he goes in to see
    what has happened to Princess Dee.
She whines, "I didn't get to snooze;
    something gave me a big bruise!"

Prince Lee jumps and bellows, "Success!
    You know, only a true princess
would be able to feel that pea,
    so please, Dee, will you marry me?"

22

The queen is glad – she jumps with joy:
"I've found a princess for my boy!"

And with the pea on royal display,
the pair get married right away.

What happens next?

Some of the pictures from the story have been mixed up! Can you retell the story and point to each picture in the correct order?

Rhyming words

Read the words in the middle of each group and point to the other words that rhyme with them.

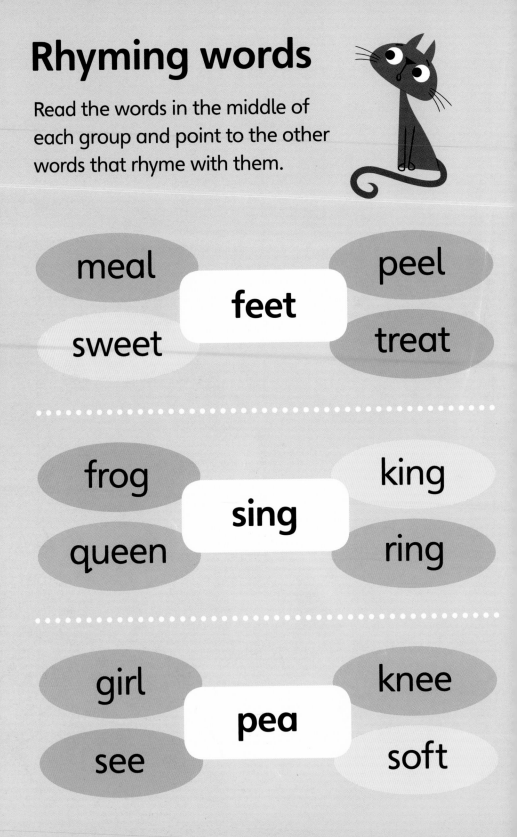

meal

peel

feet

sweet

treat

frog

king

sing

queen

ring

girl

knee

pea

see

soft

crown

head

bed

prince

red

best

grain

rain

pain

post

floor

made

door

poor

sleep

Now choose a word and make up a rhyming chant!

My **sweet feet** smell like a **treat!**

Key words

These sentences use common words to describe the story. Read the sentences and then make up new sentences for the other words in the border.

Prince Lee wanted **a** wife.

The queen **went** to see the girls.

The girls were **not** good enough.

They **saw** a girl in the rain.

The girl was **called** Dee.

like · very

· his · but · saw · with · all · we · called · are · an · not

They **made** a tall bed.

They **put** a pea in the bed.

Dee **could** not sleep.

The prince and princess **got** married.

The pea was **on** display.

the · and · a · to · no · in · he · I · of · it · went · got · they · on · she · is · for · at

could · when · there · put · this · made · so · be ·

Picture dictionary

Look carefully at the pictures and the words.
Now cover the words, one at a time.
Can you remember how to write them?

bed

bruise

door

feet

night

pea

prince

rain

teeth